ALMIGHTY

THE THIRD WORLD AMERICA SAGA

PART ONE

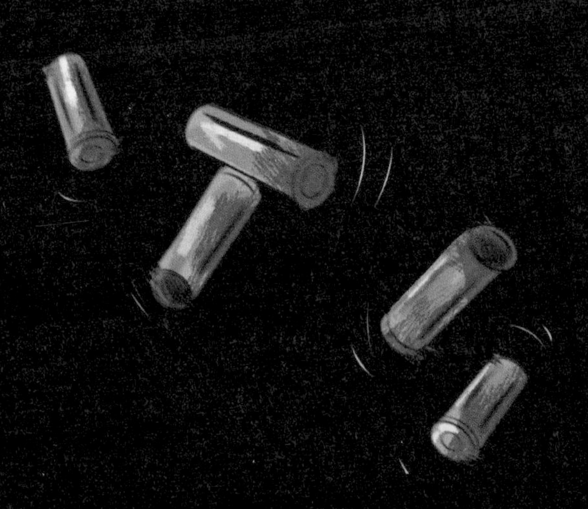

ALMIGHTY, VOL. 1. First printing. September 2023. Published by Image Comics, Inc. Office of publication: PO BOX 14457, Portland, OR 97293. Printed in Canada. For international rights, contact: foreignlicensing@imagecomics.com. ISBN: 978-1-5343-9967-9.

CHAPTER ONE

2059. AFTER DECADES OF INTERNECINE CIVIL WAR, A CATASTROPHIC ENVIRONMENTAL DISASTER ON THE AMERICAN WEST COAST BRINGS ALL FACTIONS TOGETHER TO CONTAIN IT.

TWENTY YEARS LATER, CONSTRUCTION ON THE **ZONE ONE** SUPER STRUCTURE, A WALL 250 METERS TALL AND 80 THOUSAND KILOMETERS LONG, BANKRUPTS AND ISOLATES THE COUNTRY FROM THE REST OF THE WORLD.

WHAT EMERGES FROM THE AFTERMATH IS A THIRD WORLD AMERICA, FRACTURED, DECENTRALIZED, AND DEPLETED OF ITS RESOURCES.

BARRICADED COMMUNITIES MAINTAINED BY PRIVATE SECURITY, PARAMILITARY STRIKE SQUADS, AND MILITIAS ARE THE ONLY SAFE REFUGE FROM ROVING MOTORCYCLE GANGS AND NARCO-TERRORISTS.

ALMIGHTY

2098. A GIRL HAS BEEN ABDUCTED, AND A KILLER HIRED TO FIND HER AND BRING HER HOME.

NOW.
NOW IS THE TIME.

IT'S BEEN HOURS.
DAYS.
I CAN'T FEEL MY HANDS ANYMORE.

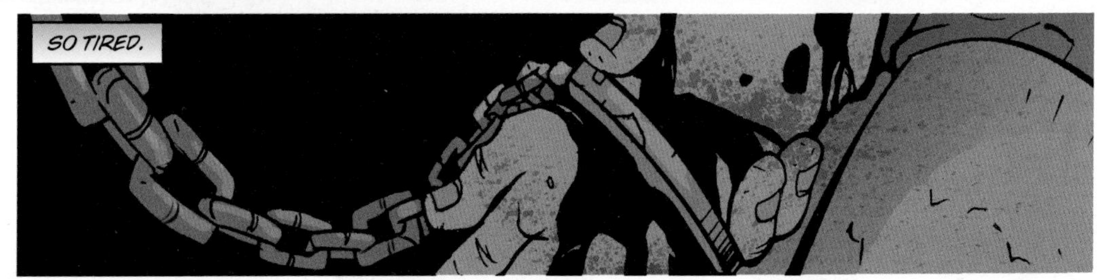
SO TIRED.

I WILL NOT DIE HERE!

THIS WILL NOT KILL ME.

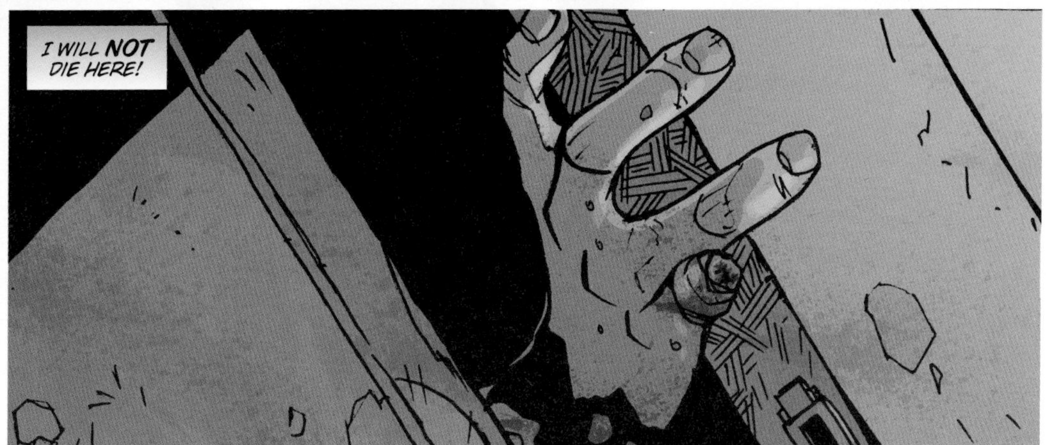
I WILL NOT DIE HERE!

THEY KNOW!

I CAN HEAR THEM!

OH, GOD. MY LEGS...
LIKE JELLY.
SO TIRED.
SO...

DEL?
DEL, HONEY. YOU FUCKED UP.
WHERE YOU GOING, HUNH?!
WHO WILL SAVE YOU?

THIS TIME, I CUT YOUR EYES OUT.

VAUGHN'S NOT HERE TO STOP ME, AND I'M HIGH AS FUCK.

SO IF I WERE YOU...

...I WOULD...

RUN!
SO TIRED. I CAN'T...
I CAN'T...

SO...
GAAHHH!
WHAT?!

MUTHAFUCKAA!
MUTHA FUCKER!
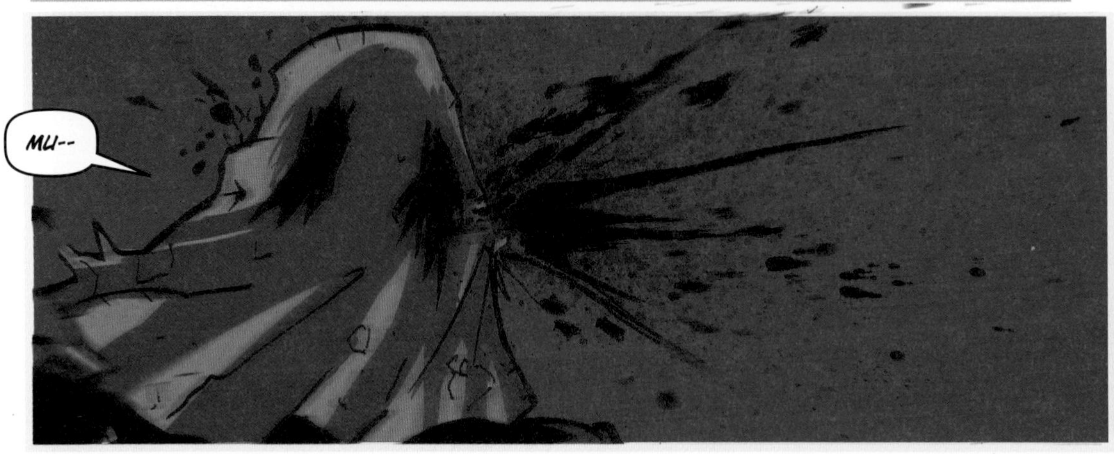
MU--

"OHHH, FUCK!
"MY HAND!
"MY GOD!

"OH, MY GOD!
"THAT'S SOME PRETTY SHIT NOW, MAN!
"OHHHAGG!

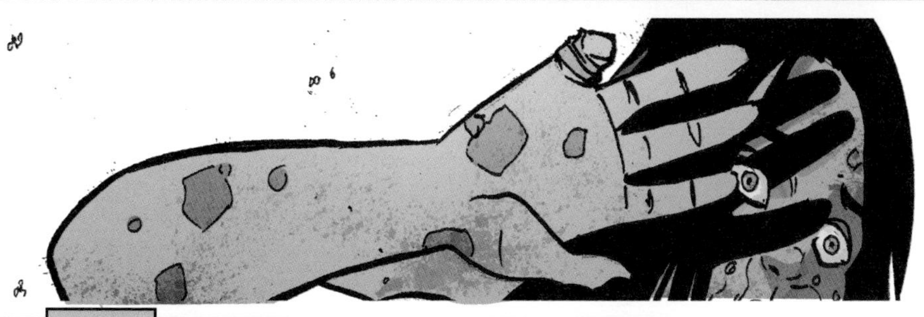

"YOU FUCKED UP.
"YOU... YOU!"

YOU BETTER KILL ME.
OH, GOD!

BITCH! YOU BETTER KILL ME!

YOU BETTER.

MY NAME IS FALE.
I'M HERE TO TAKE YOU HOME.

YOU SHOULD TRY TO GET SOME REST. WE GOT A LONG RIDE AHEAD.

I HAVE ANTIBIOTICS...A FULL RAPE KIT WITH ANTIRETRO VIRALS.

NO, THEY DIDN'T RAPE ME.

HERE.

THOSE CUTS AROUND YOUR WRIST AND THE PINKY.

IN THIS HEAT -- MIGHT GET NASTY.

THANK YOU.

NOT THAT FAR FROM 135. WE'LL LAY DOWN A *FALSE* TRAIL...

...JUST IN CASE.

CROSS THE LUCERN...HEAD *EAST* TOWARD THE *CITY*.

I'M LOW ON *FOOD* AND *FUEL*.

WEEK, *TWO* WEEKS TOPS...

I'LL GET YOU *HOME*. I *PROMISE* YOU THAT.

HOME?

BY THE TIME MY ROTATION WAS UP, I WAS HAVING A HARD TIME **FAKING** IT.

I HITCH A RIDE WITH A SUPPLY TRUCKER NAMED PHIL.
HE'S TAKING ONE OF THE SAFER ROUTES THROUGH THE NORTHERN HIGH DESERT.
PHIL'S THE KIND OF GUY WHO PROBABLY DID A LOT OF BAD THINGS IN HIS LIFE...
...'TIL HE FOUND SOMETHING BIGGER.
JESUS
GLORY

YOU JUST HAVE TO LOOK...
...IT'S ALL IN THE BOOK...THE WORD...IT'S ALL FORETOLD...

...THE ECONOMIC COLLAPSE...
...THE ASSASSINATION OF PRESIDENT HAUTHER --GOD REST HIS SOUL-- ZONE ONE. ZONE TWO. I MEAN, THESE ARE THE SIGNS!

IT HAPPENED. IT'S HAPPENING. THE END. PARADISE IS RIGHT AROUND THE CORNER.
I'M NOT MAKING THIS UP. THIS IS NOT MY OPINION. THIS IS FACT.

PARADISE!

AIN'T THAT RIGHT, BOBBY?

MISSIONARIES!
LOOKS LIKE WE GOT CHRISTIANS... OR SOMETHIN'. THEY ALWAYS GOT THE SWAG.

YEAH. RIGHT. LIKE WHAT, WARLOCK? WATER? FUEL?
FUCK IF I KNOW, VORHEES! ONLY ONE WAY TO FIND OUT FOR SURE. VAUGHN?

IT'S GETTING LATE, VORHEES. YOU THINK YOU CAN STOP THAT RIG? WITH MINIMUM DAMAGE?

IS A FROG'S ASS WATERTIGHT? SHIT, I CAN BE GENTLE.

I LOVE THIS PART.

DO YOU BELIEVE, DEL?
NOT AT THE MOMENT... NO.
"IF NOT FOR THE THREAT OF HELL OR THE PROMISE OF HEAVEN."
GOTTA BELIEVE IN SOMETHING.
BELIEF IS THE ONLY THING THAT SEPARATES MAN FROM ANIMAL.
SHIT! PHIL!
JESUS
OH, GOD!

PHIL!
CAN YOU HEAR ME?!
I THINK I SMELL GAS!

PHIL?!
JESUS, VORHEES! GENTLE LIKE A RHINO.
PLEASE... THERE ARE PEOPLE HURT IN HERE.
YEAH, BABY. I KNOW. WE'RE THE ONES THAT HURT 'EM.
IT DON'T MATTER...NONE OF THAT MATTERS NOW. IN A FEW WEEKS...
YOU'LL KNOW THEY WERE THE LUCKY ONES.

I DON'T REMEMBER THE RIDE THAT MUCH. IT FELT LIKE WE DROVE FOR **HOURS**.
MY SIDE HURT PRETTY BAD, AND I'M PRETTY SURE I ALMOST BIT MY TONGUE OFF.
I REMEMBER.

THERE WAS A HOUSE ON A HILL.

AND A SOUND...

..IN THE **WIND**.

PLEASE GOD NO!

THAT'S IT FOR THE CHOW. WE'LL HAVE THE REST FOR BREAKFAST.

IT'S PROTEIN BARS 'TIL WE RESUPPLY.

IT'LL BE A LONG RIDE. WON'T HAVE TOO MANY STOPS. TOO DANGEROUS.

LOOKS LIKE ONE OF THOSE GUYS WAS GOLDEN STATE. THEY RUN THE WHOLE AREA.
WE SHOULD BE OKAY IF WE STAY OFF THE MAIN HIGHWAY.

ONCE WE HIT THE CITY, IT GETS HARDER TO TRACK US.
GET SOME SLEEP. WE ROLL AT THE CRACK OF--

--AWW, SHIT! HERE WE GO.
LOOKS LIKE WE FOUND 'EM.

UNFUCKINBELIEVABLE. WARLOCK WENT AND GOT HIMSELF KILLED.

SHIT! WHAT KINDA BALLS YOU GOTTA HAVE FOR THAT, MANNY?

ICE...YA GOTTA HAVE BALLS OF ICE. LIKE TWO ICEBERGS RUBBIN' TOGETHER.

HOW MUCH {SNORT!} YOU BENCH, GEDDY?

140, 145 ON A GOOD DAY, STRIKE.

SNIFF-
YEAH, SNIFF
14O? HUMPH
WHAT'S UP?

NO VAUGHN, NOT EVEN HIS BIKE, BUT WE FOUND VORHEES, CALEB, AND YOUR BROTHER ...ALL SHOT TO DEATH.

THE WARLOCK?

WE FOUND TRACKS HEADING NORTH, SOME KIND OF MODIFIED BIKE...
HERNANDEZ AND ESCOBAR ARE ON IT.

GEDDY! I WANT THE MANGY FILTH THAT HAS DONE THIS TERRIBLE THING...
...THIS SAD ANIMAL, I WILL GRIND UNDER THE HEEL OF MY BOOT!

I'LL HAVE DANNI AND HIS BOYS SWEEP TOWARDS THE CITY.

WARLOCK...

MY BROTHER.

FIND HIM, GEDDY! AND I WILL HAVE HIM. I WILL HAVE HIM!

November 19, 2098.

WE STARTED EARLY...JUST LIKE FALE SAID.
IMPERIAL
BREAKFAST.
COULDN'T TELL THE DIFFERENCE BETWEEN THE BEEF AND THE AU JUS...
...BUT AFTER WEEKS OF GRILLED CHEESE AND STALE BEER, IT DIDN'T MATTER.
FALE CHANGED THE DRESSING ON MY PINKY...
...AND WE WERE READY TO GO.
FALE...
AND HER STRANGE EYES.
LUX

WE RODE THE INTERSTATE FOR ABOUT AN HOUR.

...THEN TOOK A DIRT PATH TURNABOUT.
45 MINUTES LATER, WE FOUND SOME SHADE UNDER A TREE.
I HAVE TO **PEE**.

GOOD. THIS'LL BE THE **LAST STOP** BEFORE NIGHTFALL.
WHERE YOU **GOING?**

TO **PEE.**

RIGHT **HERE.** DON'T WANDER OFF.

I DON'T THINK I CAN GO WITH YOU **WATCHING.**

SERIOUSLY?

I KNOW. IT'S STUPID.

TOO DANGEROUS.

THERE'S NO ONE AROUND FOR MILES.

THAT DOESN'T MEAN IT'S SAFE. LOOK, I CAN ONLY GUARANTEE YOUR SAFETY IF YOU DO EXACTLY AS I SAY.
DO NOT HESITATE. DO NOT DEVIATE, AND I WILL GET YOU HOME.

RIGHT.

FINE.

BETTER?
YUP.

WHAT'S THE PROBLEM, ESCOBAR? WHY ARE WE STOPPING?

HERNANDEZ THINKS WE'RE ON THE WRONG TRACK.
WHOEVER WASTED WARLOCK RODE OFF ON A MOD.

SO.

NOT ENOUGH FUEL TO GET ANYWHERE WORTH A DAMN, GEDDY.
AT LEAST NOT IN THIS DIRECTION.

...

HERNANDEZ WANTS TO DOUBLE BACK AND CHECK FOR FIRE ROADS.

DO IT!

EVERY MAN TO HIS TASK, GEDDY. THE OLD MAN KNOWS HIS BUSINESS.

TWO ROWS ON EACH SIDE OF THE HIGHWAY.
MOVE!

CHAPTER TWO

WE'RE MAKIN' GOOD TIME. SHOULD HIT LONCAST BY NOON.
HATE THAT FUCKIN' CITY. MUCH TOO CLOSE TO ZONE ONE FOR MY TASTE.

HERE.

DINNER?

WHAT, YOU DON'T LIKE LEMONPEPPER CHICKEN WITH BABY POTATOES?

FALE, HOW DID YOU FIND ME?
I RAN INTO ONE OF THEM AT A BAR. HE WAS DRUNK.

AND HE WAS TRYING TO UNLOAD SOME OF THE SWAG FROM THE WRECK.

I GOT LUCKY. I GOT HIM OUTSIDE. OUT BACK.

WE CAME TO AN UNDERSTANDING... HE TALKED AND GAVE UP YOUR LOCATION.
AND MY AUNT?

AFTER YOU DIDN'T SHOW FROM YOUR ROTATION WITH AID CORP...
...YOUR AUNT AND FRIENDS TRIED TO SEARCH FOR YOU.

THEY FOUND THE RIG, BUT THEY DIDN'T FIND YOUR BODY.

THEY FIGURED MAYBE SLAVERS GOT YOU, OR COYOTES DRAGGED YOU INTO THE HILLS.

DEAD OR ALIVE, THEY JUST WANTED TO KNOW. ONE WAY OR THE OTHER.

HMM.

WHAT?

DUST CLOUD.
YEAH... WHAT'S THAT MEAN?

WE'RE BEING FOLLOWED.

AGAIN?!

NOW WHAT, ESCOBAR?

IT'S NOT A GOOD IDEA TO CONTINUE, GEDDY. ROAD GETS PRETTY ROUGH. MIGHT END UP IN A GULLY, ALL BUSTED

WHOEVER WE'RE TRACKING HAS PROBABLY DONE THE SAME.
DON'T WORRY. HERNANDEZ HAS THEIR TRACE.

ALL RIGHT.
OLD MAN HAS THEIR *TRACE*. WHAT IF THEY KEEP MOVING AT *NIGHT?*

DON'T MATTER. WE'RE TRAVELING NORTHEAST. WE *KNOW* WHERE THEY'RE HEADED.

REALLY, *WHERE?*

LONCAST CITY.

DANNI AND HIS BOYS ARE PROBABLY ROLLING IN THERE NOW.
WE *GOT* THEM. WE GOT THEM BOXED *IN!*

NO TIME FOR BREAKFAST. THE IDEA OF GETTING BACK ON THAT BIKE FOR THE NEXT COUPLE OF HOURS JUST KILLED ME.

WE RESTED AFTER A WHILE.
HMM.
WHAT?

LOTTA VEHICLES. MUSTA DROPPED SOMEONE IMPORTANT.

I DOUBT IT.

SHOULDN'T BE TOO HARD TO TRACK US.
HAVEN'T BEEN COVERING OUR TRACKS SINCE WE DOUBLED BACK.

DOESN'T MATTER. WE'LL HIT **LONCAST** BEFORE THEY CATCH UP.
STILL, MAYBE I CAN RIG SOMETHING UP THAT'LL SLOW 'EM DOWN.

I DON'T THINK I'D EVER BEEN SO HAPPY TO SEE A PAVED ROAD IN MY LIFE.
100

FALE FLIPPED A LEVER AND HER BIKE SHIFTED AND STRETCHED OUT UNDER US.

TEARS STREAMED DOWN MY FACE AS WE RACED DOWN THE ROAD.
CITY

ON THE HORIZON, THE CITY AND THE WALLS OF **ZONE ONE**.

"IF NOT FOR THE THREAT OF HELL OR THE PROMISE OF HEAVEN.'
"GOTTA BELIEVE IN SOMETHING.
GASMART
Z
"BELIEF'S THE ONLY THING THAT SEPARATES MAN--
GAS MART
Z

"FROM ANIMAL."
THIS'LL TIDE YOU OVER 'TIL DINNER.

I KNOW A PLACE WE CAN GRAB A SHOWER AND GET SOME REST.

A SHOWER?

PARADISE.

DID YOU FIND IT?

PHIL, THE SUPPLY TRUCKER WAS RIGHT ABOUT ONE THING, BELIEF IS FOR PEOPLE.

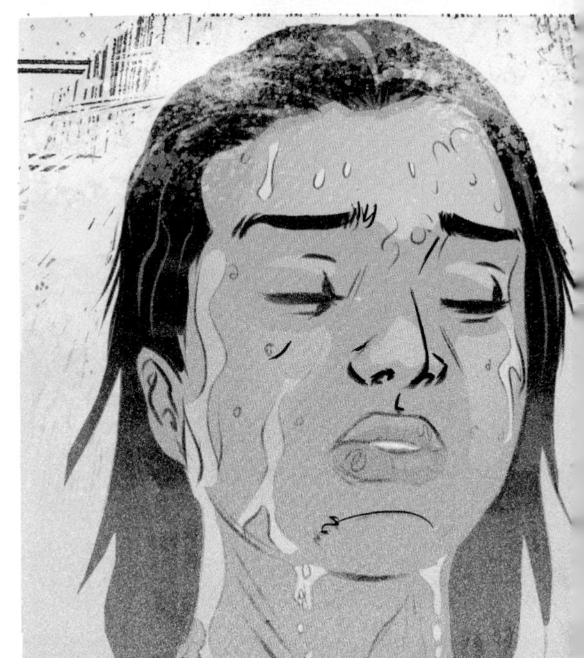

I GUESS I'M HAVING A HARD TIME BELIEVING IN PEOPLE RIGHT NOW.

SHOWER'S ALL YOURS.

FALE?

UHHF.

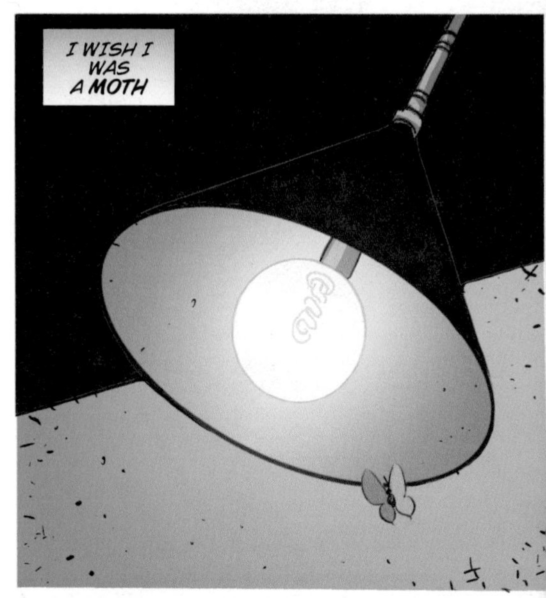
I WISH I WAS A MOTH

WITHOUT A CARE IN THE WORLD.

WANTING NOTHING, EXCEPT FOR THE LIGHT.

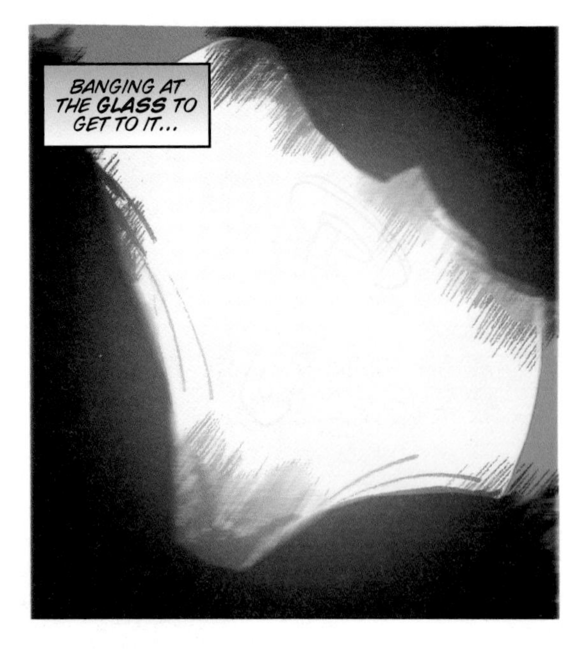
BANGING AT THE GLASS TO GET TO IT...

...EVEN THOUGH IT'LL BURN ME.

WHAT THE HELL WAS THAT?

IT FELT LIKE THE DREAM OF A MEMORY--

--THAT HASN'T HAPPENED YET.
HUNGRY?

"STARVING."

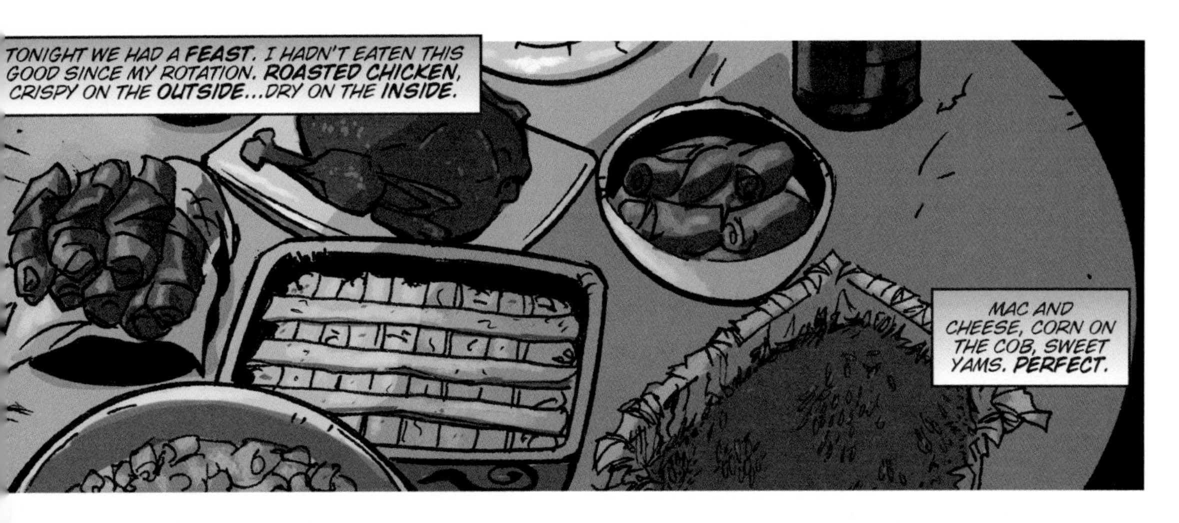
TONIGHT WE HAD A FEAST. I HADN'T EATEN THIS GOOD SINCE MY ROTATION. ROASTED CHICKEN, CRISPY ON THE OUTSIDE...DRY ON THE INSIDE.
MAC AND CHEESE, CORN ON THE COB, SWEET YAMS. PERFECT.

FALE? CAN I ASK YOU A PERSONAL QUESTION?
SURE.

YOUR EYES... HOW ARE THEY LIKE THAT?! I MEAN, I'VE NEVER SEEN ANYONE...
I WAS BORN IN ZONE ONE NEAR IXION.

BORN IN ZONE ONE? NOW THAT'S--
I MEAN, ARE THERE PEOPLE STILL LIVING IN ZONE ONE?
SATAN

NO. NOT PEOPLE.

THINGS. THINGS LIVE IN ZONE ONE NOW.

HEY, YOU WANT TO GET A DRINK?
I COULD DRINK RIGHT NOW.

UH... YEAH, ME TOO..
GOOD. I KNOW A PLACE NOT TOO FAR FROM HERE.

...WITH A SMALL DANCE FLOOR.

FREAKS, NOMADS, PROTOINDUSTRIALISTS...

ALL TRYING TO ERASE THE DAY.

FALE POURED THE FIRST ROUND.

THE GOOD STUFF.

...STRONG, BITTER FIRE.

BETTER THAN THE SHINE WE DISTILLED AT AID CORP.

GETCHA ANYTHING ELSE, FALE?

YEAH. HERE, DIDI.

MAKE SURE BELLA GETS THIS, AND LEAVE THE BOTTLE.
UH, SURE, FALE. SURE THING.
UH...SO, WE'RE NOT GONNA HAVE ANY PROBLEMS TONIGHT. YEAH, FALE?
NAH. NOT TONIGHT, DIDI. NOT FROM ME.
NOT FROM ME.

I'M ALIVE.

BUMPING UP AGAINST THE LIGHT LIKE A MOTH, BUT I'M ALIVE..

THANKS TO HER.

I GUESS THAT'S NOT MUCH OF A SURPRISE.

THIS MUST BE BELLA.

FALE'S KEY.

I'D NEVER BEEN THIS CLOSE TO IT BEFORE.

HEY.

HEY, LADY.
HEY, *FOX*.

HEHE.

GOD DAMN! THIS WHITE BITCH IS GOTH!
HEY, DANNI...I THINK WE GOT OUR PILOT HERE.

HSV KODIAC, HARD BORE MAGNA SERIES.

WOW.

NICE BIKE.

OH, MY GOD! ARE THESE THE GUYS FOLLOWING US?

LET'S SEE.
GOLDEN STATE.

IF I KEEP *KILLING* THESE PEOPLE, SOMEONE'S *BOUND* TO TAKE *OFFENSE*.

RIGHT *THERE!*

BE *COOL!* I *GOT* YOU, OKAY? BE *REAL COOL!*

MILITIA.

YOUR HANDS! LET ME SEE YOUR HANDS!

LISTEN...I'M ON A RETRIEVE AND PROTECT OP...
...I'M LISTED FALE RED ONE NINER.

DID YOU JUST KILL THESE PEOPLE?

HERE WE GO.

SHOTS FIRED! SHOTS FIRED! 10-13 IN THE ALLEY BEHIND BELLAS.

WHOA! WHOA! WHO SAID YOU COULD PUT YOUR ARMS DOWN?!
I SA

WE'RE NOT DOING THIS.

FALE, HE'S A COP. MAYBE...

YOUR WEAPONS!
HAND THEM OVER...HANDLE FIRST!
THAT'S NOT HAPPENING.

LOOK, YOU JUST WASTED **FOUR** PEOPLE. I'M NOT SAYING IT **WASN'T** SELF-DEFENSE...

...WHAT I AM SAYING IS YOU'VE GOT FIVE SECONDS TO HAND OVER YOUR **SIDEARM**.

FALE, **WAIT**. UM...

MAYBE WE--

BITCH, I'M NOT LYING. I WILL SHOOT YOU IN THE FACE!

ARE YOU FAST?
ARE YOU LUCKY?

BE COOL, GODDAMN IT. BE--

LMC
YOU HAVE TO BE BOTH, TO KILL ME.

HOLD ON... JUST LET ME GET THIS OFF YOU.

FALE, WE CAN'T JUST--
LEAVE IT!

JUST *LEAVE IT!*

MAYBE IF HE'S *LUCKY*, HIS BACKUP WILL GET HERE IN TIME.

COME ON.

CHAPTER THREE

WE GOT TEN MINUTES...

17

LCM's GONNA LOCK DOWN THIS WHOLE FUCKIN' CITY.

17

WOULDN'T HAVE COME BACK HERE IF WE DIDN'T ABSOLUTELY NEED THIS SHIT.

STEP AWAY FROM THE GODDAMN WINDOW, DEL!

LISTEN! BEFORE THIS THING'S OVER, CHANCES ARE YOU'RE GONNA SEE SOME CRAZY SHIT.
BUT I PROMISE YOU...

STAY LOW, MOVE FAST.

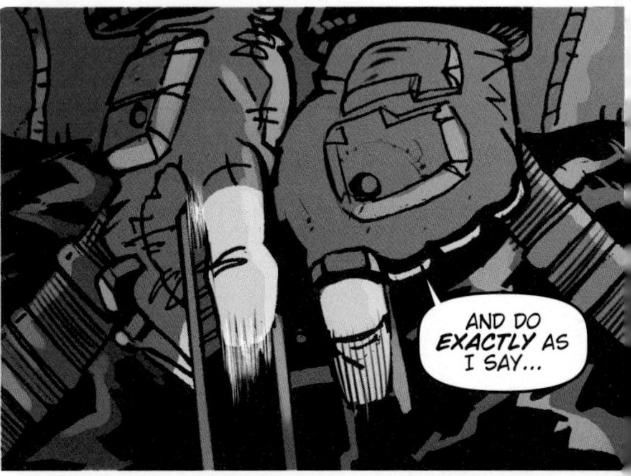
AND DO EXACTLY AS I SAY...

...AND I'LL GET YOU HOME.
FALE--
LUX

CAN WE STOP SHOOTING COPS?
I DOUBT IT. THESE GUYS AREN'T COPS, DEL. THEY'RE MILITIA.

THE WORLD'S A BETTER PLACE *WITHOUT* HIM.

BELIEVE ME.

THE *LONCAST MILITIA CORPS* IS JUST AS BAD AS *GOLDEN STATE*.

MAYBE EVEN WORSE.

UH...

THINK *FAST!*

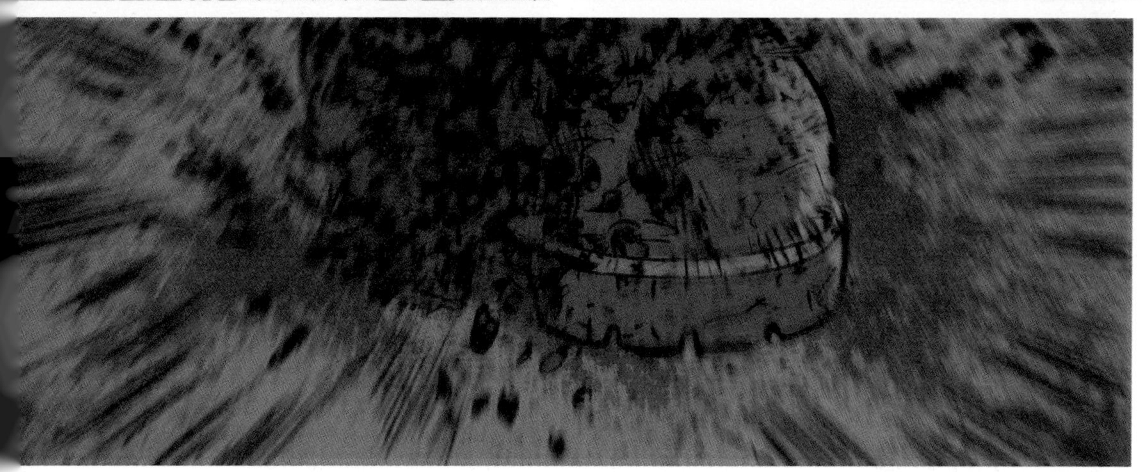

OH, SWEET JESUS!
NO FEAR!

FREEZE!

GODDAMMIT, I SAID FREEZE!
NO FEAR

LUX

FALL BACK!
FALL BACK!
NINE, NINE, NINE... ON ME!

OH, GOD!

THE DOOR! TAKE THE CHAIR AND BARRICADE THE DOOR!

QUICKLY! DO IT NOW!
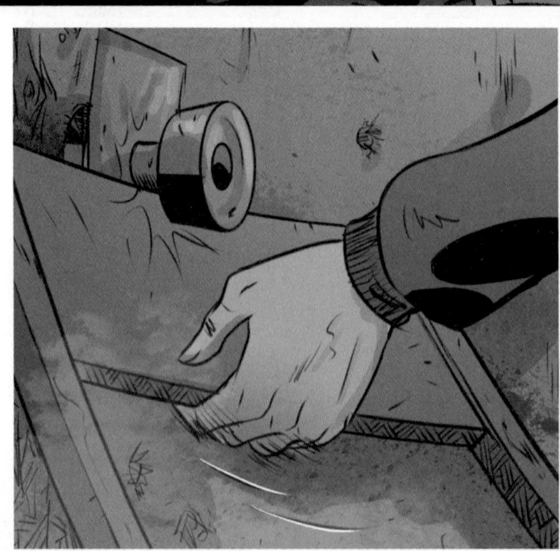

GOOD. REMEMBER WHAT I SAID.

STAY LOW, MOVE FAST!

HERE.

ANYONE TRIES TO GET THROUGH THAT DOOR, MAKE A HOLE IN IT.

ANDERS IS DOWN. I TOLD YOU WE SHOULDA WAITED FOR BACKUP!
GET YOUR ASS IN THERE, PAUL. KILL EVERYTHING IN THAT ROOM!
EMBER AMPHION!!
LMC

DEL, GET THAT VEST ON.

CAUGHT THEM OFF GUARD.

SANCHEZ! CGR THROUGH THE FUCKIN' WINDOW... MOVE!
LMC

THEY'RE GONNA TRY TO BOX US IN.

THEY'RE OFF **BALANCE**. WE GOTTA HIT HARD, WITH **SPEED**...

AND OVERWHELMING **FIREPOWER!**
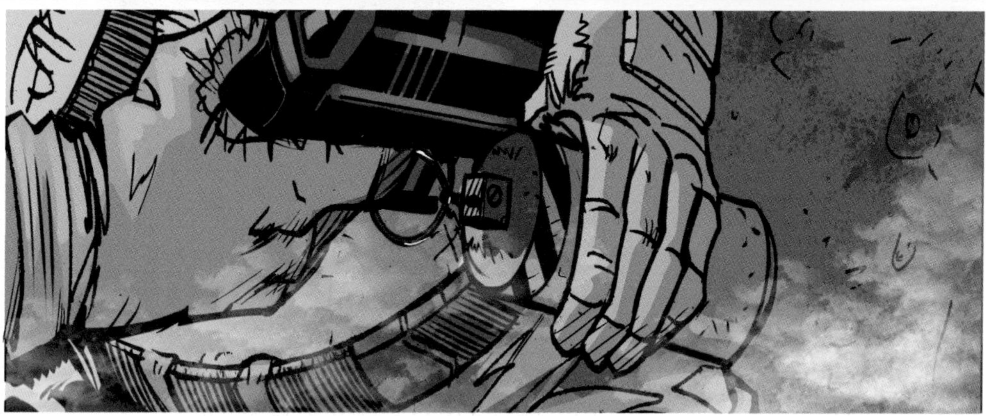

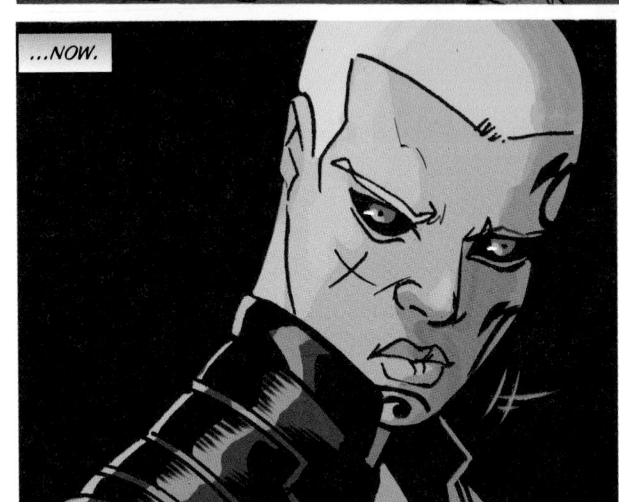
...NOW.

I'M HIT!

NOW IS THE TIME.

MIKE, THE CGR!

OH, MAN. THIS IS GONNA SU--
LMC

IT'S BEEN HOURS...DAYS.

I CAN'T HEAR MYSELF SCREAM.

SO TIRED...
LMC

THERE MUST HAVE BEEN MORE TO FALE THAN JUST HER BIZARRE EYES.

SHE COULD MOVE FASTER THAN I COULD SEE.

AND SHE WAS STRONGER THAN SHE LOOKED, 'CAUSE I WAS STILL REELING FROM THE EXPLOSION.

BUT FALE?

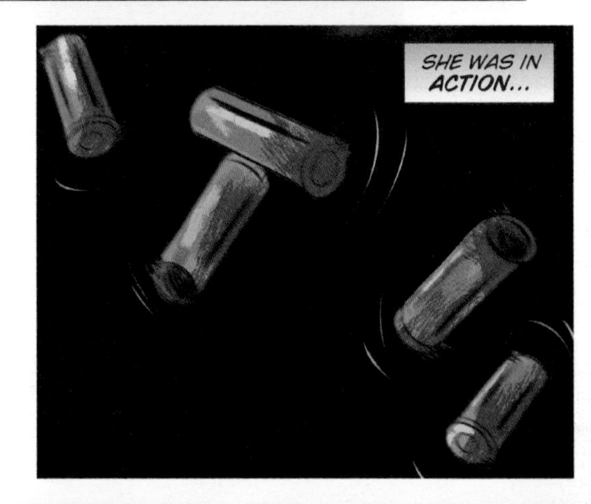
SHE WAS IN ACTION...

...ALL PURPOSE AND WILL.

...A KILLER OF MEN.

AND SHE WAS GOOD AT IT.

GET READY TO MOVE!

THEY'RE FALLING BACK.

017
GRAB THE DUFFLE. STAY CLOSE.

OKAY. WE'RE MOVING.

FUCK ME... HUNH?!

FUCK YOU, BITCH!

AHHHKK!
SHIT!

UH, SHIT!

THAT FUCKIN' HURTS.

WHOA!

GET BEHIND ME!

HEAD FOR THE ***TRANSPO***. I'LL COVER YOU.

RICOCHET GOT ME!

WON'T GET TOO FAR LIKE THIS.

FALE, WE STILL HAVE THE MED KIT.

I THINK I CAN STOP THE BLEEDING...

BUT WE HAVE TO FIND SOMEPLACE SAFE.

I HAVE A BAD IDEA.

ZONE ONE, SHE SAID.
DELPHION GATE

EVER SINCE THE **ECONOMIC COLLAPSE**, SECURITY ON THE WALL HAD BEEN WEAK. **FALE** SAID SHE KNEW A WAY IN.
DANGER
RD-12 CAST ZED
NO WAY OUT
IT WILL BE **DANGEROUS**, SHE SAID

BUT EVEN IF THEY FOUND THE CAR....

...AND KNEW WHERE WE WENT...
LUX

THEY WOULD HAVE TO BE A SPECIAL KIND OF **CRAZY**...

...TO FOLLOW US.

THIS IS OUR GUY. AFTER WASTING DANNI AND HIS BOYS, HE CAME HERE... ROOM 17.

LCM HAD THEM PINNED, BUT THEY SHOT THEIR WAY OUT AND STOLE ONE OF THE HEAVY TRANSPORTS.

YEAH, WE'RE GETTING CHATTER. THEY FOUND THE APC AT A WATER TREATMENT PLANT NEAR DELPHION GATE.

AMAELL. LET'S GO. WE'RE GETTING CLOSER NOW.

ONE OF 'EM HIT PRETTY GOOD.
LOOKS LIKE THOSE CRAZY FUCKERS WENT OFF INTO THIS CHANNEL... ONTO THE OTHER SIDE OF ZONE ONE.

GET WET.

BUT STRIKE...

THEY'RE AS GOOD AS DEAD... IF THEY'RE LUCKY.
DEAD?

THE ONLY DEAD I KNOW ABOUT FOR SURE IS MY BROTHER AND SEVEN OF MY CREW.
AND THE SLIPPERY FUCK RESPONSIBLE FOR THAT IS CLOSE...

CHAPTER FOUR

IT WAS CLOSE.

EVEN WITH A BATTLEFIELD MED KIT AND MY AID CORP TRAINING. I WASN'T SURE IF SHE WAS GOING TO MAKE IT.
BUT THE BULLET WAS OUT, AND SHE WAS RESPONDING WELL TO THE PATCH FOAM.

THE ONLY THING WAS THAT SHE HAD A HIGH FEVER, AND IT WASN'T GOING TO BREAK WITHOUT HELP.

AND IF I WANTED TO GET OUT OF HERE ALIVE...

FALE WAS GOING TO HAVE TO LEAD THE WAY.

SOME OF THE THINGS I'D HEARD ABOUT THIS PLACE SOUNDED **TOO** STRANGE TO BE TRUE.

TOO **INCREDIBLE.**

THEY SAID SOMETHING HAD HAPPENED HERE A LONG TIME AGO.
AN ACCIDENT.

THEY TRIED TO CONTAIN IT...

PHARMACY
50%
...BUT IT KEPT GROWING.

LMC
NOMI
PERFECT.
LMC
NOW I JUST GOTTA MAKE IT BACK.

I WAS A COUPLE OF BLOCKS AWAY WHEN I HEARD IT.
A FLUTTERING SOUND.

INSECT WINGS.

I HAD HEARD IT BEFORE IN MY DREAM.

IT LOOKED LIKE A LITTLE BOY, BUT EVERY CELL IN MY BODY KNEW IT WASN'T.
UM... HELLO?

AND EVERY CELL IN MY BODY WANTED TO RUN.

PLAY?

LMC

PLAY?

OH, GOD.
LMC

FUCK!

FUCK! FUCK! FUCK!

SHIT!

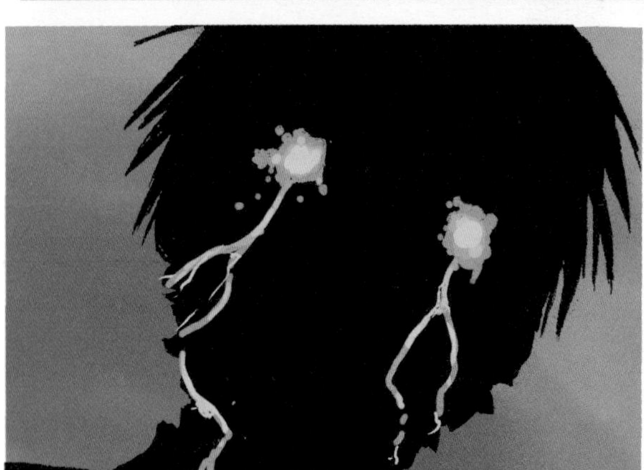

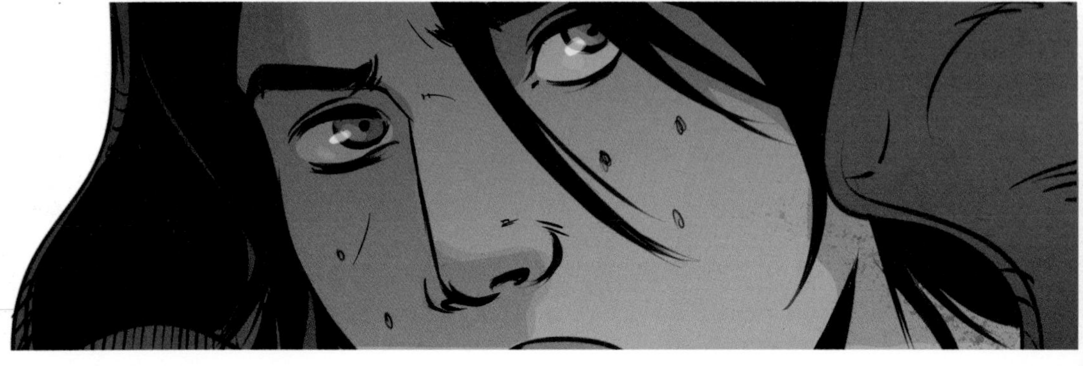

WHOA! EASY, NOW. EASY!

QUIET NOW. KEEP *QUIET*.

IT CAN'T SEE.

IT'S *BLIND*.

OKAY, IT'S MOVING *OFF*.

WHAT THE HELL *WAS* THAT?!
ABOMONOG! HEH.
LMC

THEY DON'T USUALLY FORAGE THIS FAR *NORTH* FROM THE *GREAT MOTHER*.

AT LEAST NOT THIS CLOSE TO *FEEDING* TIME.

I WAS A SCIENTIST. A BOTANIST. MY TEAM AND I WERE IN CHARGE OF CATALOGING NOVEL PLANT LIFE NEAR AMPHION.

I WAS THERE WHEN THE GREAT MOTHER FIRST SPROUTED...
...THE FIRST TO TASTE ITS MILK.

I KNOW WHAT YOU'RE THINKING. IT'S SHOCKING WHEN YOU FIRST SEE THEM, I GET THAT.

THE ABOMONOG? HER DRONES? EVERYONE THINKS THEY'RE ZOMBIES, BUT THEY'RE NOT.

THEY'RE SO MUCH MORE THAN THAT. ALL THEY WANT IS THE MILK AND ALL IT WANTS IS TO BE MILKED.
IT'S THE PERFECT OUTCOME FOR AN UNFORTUNATE SITUATION, *YES*, VERY UNFORTUNATE.

UH HUH.

LOOK, UM... *THANKS* AGAIN FOR HELPING ME *OUT* BACK THERE...

...AND SAVING ME FROM THE UM--

THE *GREAT MOTHER*.

THAT'S SO *FUNNY*. YOU DON'T *BELIEVE* ME.

IMF

YOU WANNA SEE SOMETHING?
PERFECTLY BALANCED LIFE? A CLOSED LOOP OF WANT AND NEED?

YOU ARE NOT GOING TO LIKE IT, IT'S UNPLEASANT. BUT YOU'LL LEARN TO LOVE IT.

YOU'LL LOVE IT LIKE A MOTH...
...LOVES FLAME.

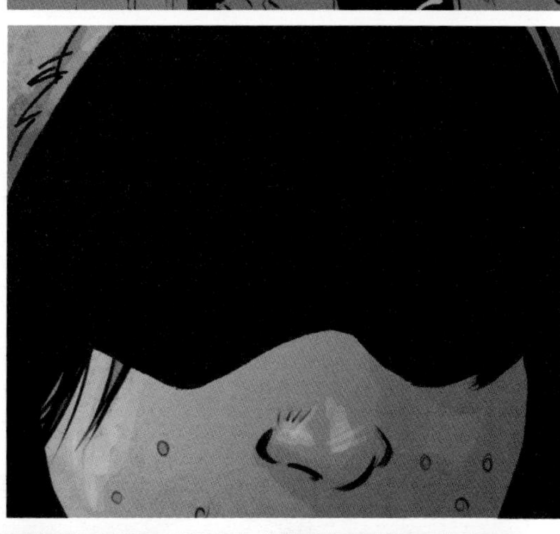

YOU'RE GOING TO BE SO HUNGRY FOR IT...
YOUR RIBS WILL BE SHOWING.

ONLY THAT GOLDEN NECTAR, THAT SWEET LIGHT...

...WILL FILL YOU.

YOU BETTER GO.

IF I START SHOOTING, I WON'T BE ABLE TO STOP.
YOU CAN'T USE THAT HERE, AT THIS TIME OF DAY? WHO KNOWS WHAT YOU'LL ATTRACT!

DEL, MY PANTS?

RIGHT BEHIND YOUR HEAD, **FALE**. HOW DO YOU FEEL?

TIGHT.
LIKE **TEN** POUNDS OF SHIT SHOVED INTO A **FIVE-POUND** BAG.

HOW LONG HAVE I BEEN **DOWN?**

IT'S BEEN A COUPLE OF **DAYS**. YOU'VE BEEN FIGHTING A NASTY **FEVER**.

THE OLD MAN?
LUX

WOW. YOU LOOK LIKE **HELL**.

YOU SHOULD HAVE RUN WHEN YOU HAD THE CHANCE, BECAUSE I'M GOING TO CHOP YOU UP INTO FIVE PIECES.
AND YOU'RE GONNA BE ALIVE WHILE I DO IT.

NOW WAIT A MINUTE... I SAVED HER. YOUR FRIEND.
THAT'S GOTTA BE WORTH SOMETHING, RIGHT?

I-- WAIT, DO YOU... HEAR THAT?
THAT SOUND.

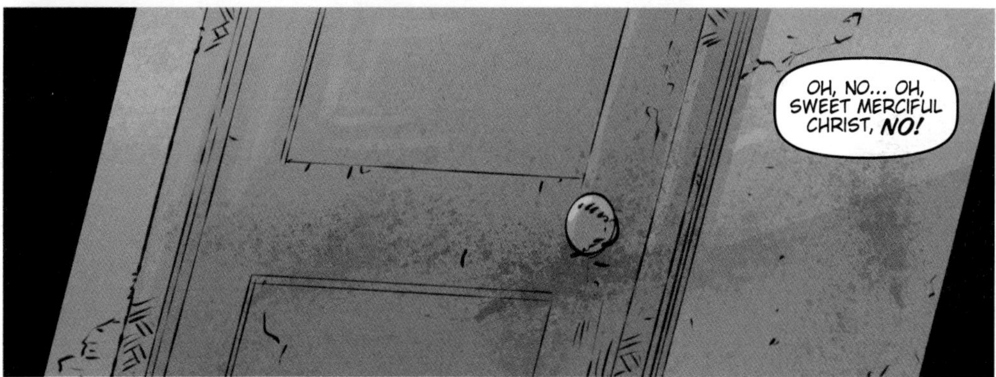
OH, NO... OH, SWEET MERCIFUL CHRIST, NO!

ABOMONOG!
IT'S HERE...

IT FOLLOWED US.

PLAY?

PLAY?

AHHAGG!
HERE!

PLAY WITH THIS!

AHH! GET IT OFF ME! PLEASE GET IT OFF ME!

NO!!
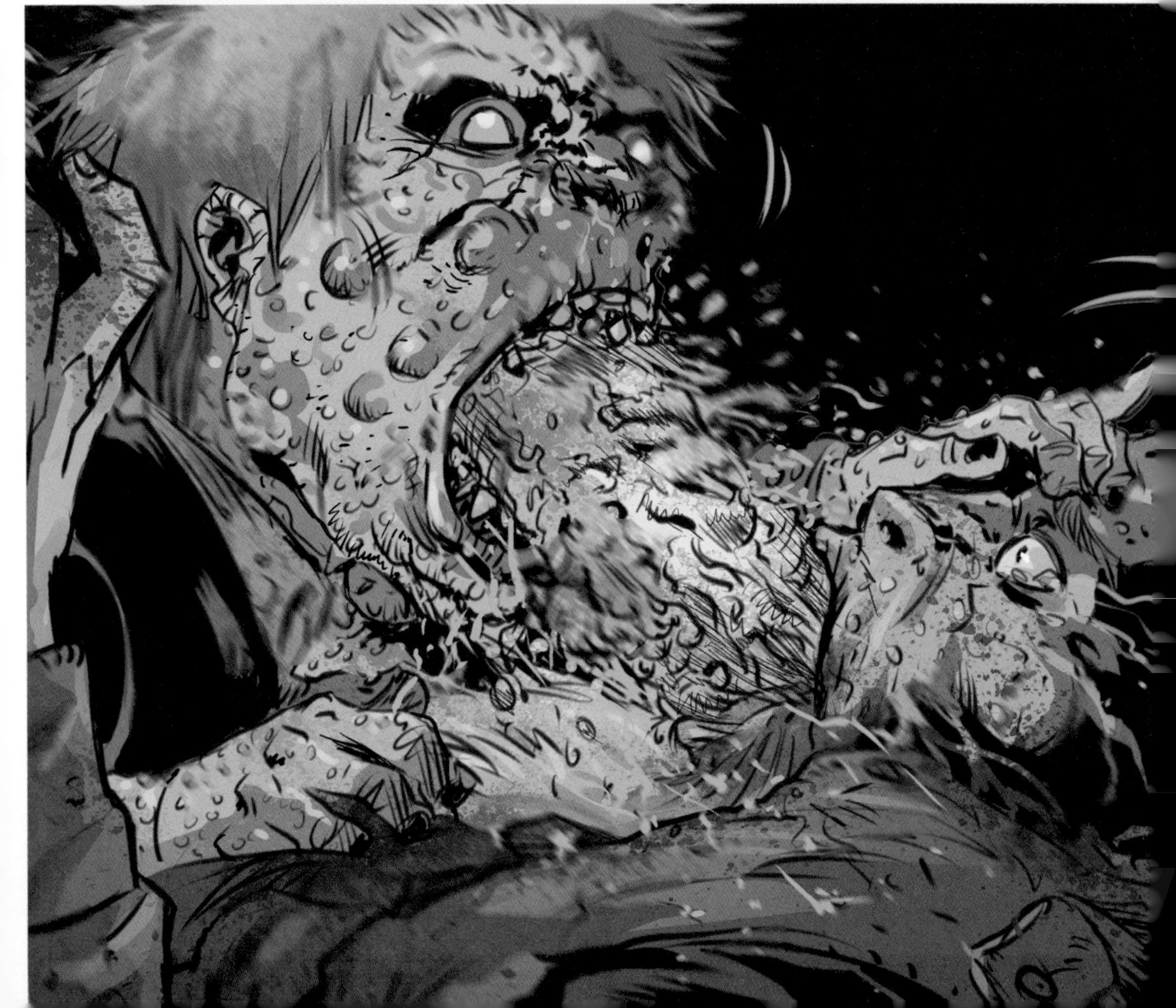

WATCH THE FLASH!

GOD DAMMIT! I HATE THIS PLACE.

WE'RE MOVING.

FALE WAS IN NO CONDITION TO MAKE IT OUT OF ZONE 1.
SHE NEEDED MORE REST.
HOOVER
HOOVER

THE DOOR.
GOT IT.

I JUST NEED TO CATCH MY BREATH...
LMC

CLOSE MY EYES FOR A FEW MINUTES, THEN I'LL GET YOU HOME. BELIEVE THAT.

SOFA KING
I DO. I BELIEVE.

THERE'S A SOUND ON THE WIND.

IT LIES DOWN CLOSE TO THE GROUND.

CHURNING.

CHANGING.
BECOMING.

FALE?

CHECK THOSE CORNERS.

WHAT'S THIS ***GLASS*** HERE?

JOHNNY, RANGE UP A CLICK. DON'T GET TOO FAR.

BOO!

SHIT!

GOTCHA!

DON'T BE SO SHY!

I KNOW A COUPLE OF US ARE ROUGH AROUND THE EDGES, AND WE COULD STAND TO SHOWER.

BUT YOU SEE, WE'VE BEEN ON THE ROAD FOR A FEW DAYS.

HERE. LET ME.

SO SOFT. SO PRETTY.

AND YOU MAKE SUCH SOFT--

AND PRETTY...

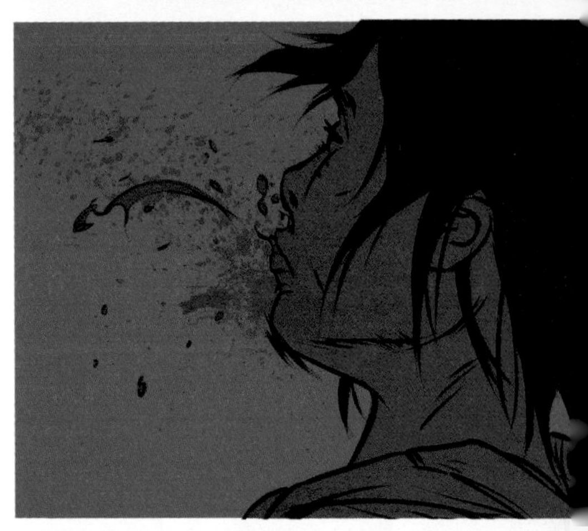

...SOUNDS!

UHH!

WAIT! STOP, PLEASE!

WHO ARE YOU PEOPLE?!

WHY ARE YOU DOING THIS?

SHH. BE QUIET.
PLEASE...

WHAT DO YOU WANT? WHO ARE YOU?

THIS CREATURE? THIS LITTLE THING?

NO... THIS CHILD DID NOT KILL MY BROTHER, WARLOCK

A MAN.

A SLAYER.

A STONE-COLD KILLER LIKE WARLOCK!

GEDDY, KILL THE GIRL! RIGHT NOW!
NO. THE TRIGGER IS STILL IN THERE... TRYING TO GET US TO GO IN, WHERE IT'S NICE AND DARK.

CHAPTER FIVE

SHOW HIM WHAT I **WANT**, GEDDY!

SHOW HIM WHAT IT'S **LIKE!**

WAIT!

HOLD ON!

WAIT!!

HOLD YOUR FIRE! HOLD YOUR FIRE!!

YOU SHOOT THOSE THINGS IN HERE AND YOU'VE JUST KILLED US!

YOU KNOW WHERE WE *ARE*?

ZONE 1!

AND IN ZONE 1, SOMETIMES DEATH IS YOUR ONE CHANCE OUT.

SO NOW PLEASE, LET'S GET A LOOK AT YOU.

...

YOU!

HOW ARE YOU ALIVE-

WHEN I FUCKIN' KILLED YOU!?!

AMAELL, WHAT...

I KNOW HER.
WE SERVED AT AMPHION-

A LONG TIME AGO.

YEAH, GOOD TIMES.
GREAT TIMES.

BETTER TIMES THAN THESE, RIGHT FALE?

I REMEMBER AMPHION, AMAELL. I REMEMBER YOU PROMISED ME WAR WITHOUT END.

WELL?

I ALWAYS HEARD YOU WERE GOOD WITH A KNIFE.

SHOW ME!
LMC

LMC

COME ON!

COME ON!!

NOW YOU'RE IN *MY* WORLD!

KNIFE!

GUN. GRAPPLE. I DON'T CARE.

TODAY IS A SPECIAL DAY.

TODAY, I SHOW YOU WHAT I'VE ALWAYS KNOWN...

THAT YOU MAY BE A KILLER- BUT I AM A WARRIOR. I SERVE SOMETHING GREATER THAN MYSELF.

MY PEOPLE! MY CREW!!

THAT'S WHAT MAKES ME STRONGER!

HONOR!

DUTY!!

SOMETHING A LONE WOLF LIKE YOU COULD NEVER UNDERSTAND-

NOW DIE!

UTTERLY ALONE AND BEATEN, AT THE END OF THE WORLD.

AHHHGG!

BORN ALONE, DIE ALONE, DOESN'T MAKE A DIFFERENCE TO ME.

YOU'RE STRONG, **AMAELL**- BUT ARE YOU **FAST?**
ARE YOU **LUCKY?**

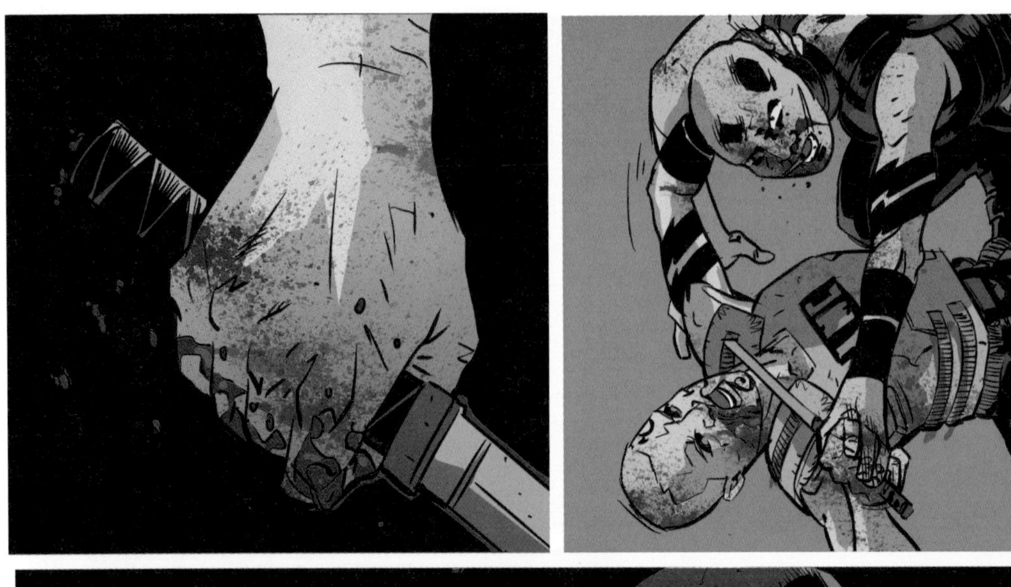

WHAT!

NO, NOT FAST ENOUGH-

NOT LUCKY ENOUGH.

YOU HAVE TO BE BOTH, IF YOU WANT TO KILL ME.

NOW LISTEN UP! I WANT THE GIRL. AND I WILL ABSOLUTELY AND WITHOUT MERCY MURDER ANY MOTHERLESS FUCK THAT GETS IN MY WAY!

YOU HEAR ME?!

YOU FUCKIN' GET THAT?!

YOU CRAZY BITCH!

YOU HAVE NO IDEA-

-OF THE POWER.

MY STRENGTH-
MY STRENGTH!

I WILL CHOKE YOU! I WILL TAKE YOU DOWN AND BREAK YOU!
WHEN I FINALLY ALLOW YOU TO DIE, YOU WILL WEEP IN ECSTASY!!

STRIKE!!

OH MY GOD!!

PLAY!

DON'T MOVE-
DON'T MAKE A
SOUND.

FALE?!

STAY
CLOSE,
DEL.
STRIKE,
WHAT DO WE
DO?

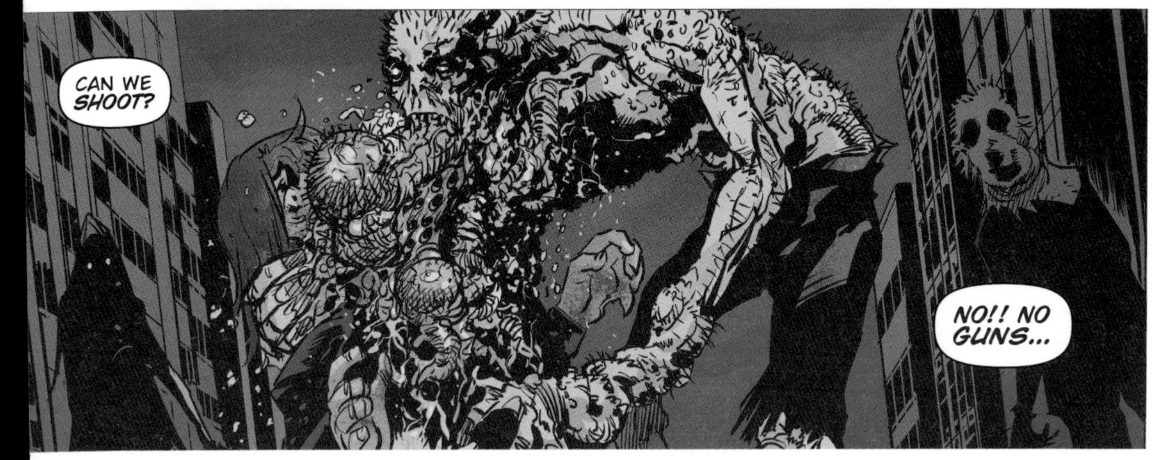
CAN WE
SHOOT?
NO!! NO
GUNS...

NO SHOOTING! IT'S ONLY THREE OF THEM. LET'S KEEP IT THAT WAY.

WE CAN- ...WE...

OH, FUCK THIS! FALL BACK! FALL BACK!!

ONE OF THE ABOMONOG POINTED- I REMEMBER THAT CLEARLY, AND THEN I FELT A PRESSURE BEHIND MY EYES.

AND A BURNT TASTE IN MY MOUTH-

THE BUZZING IN MY HEAD WAS SO LOUD.

IT WAS CHAOS, AND PEOPLE STARTED TO DROP WHERE THEY STOOD.

SLEEP!
RUN!

LIKE SOMEONE JUST TURNED OFF THE LIGHTS.

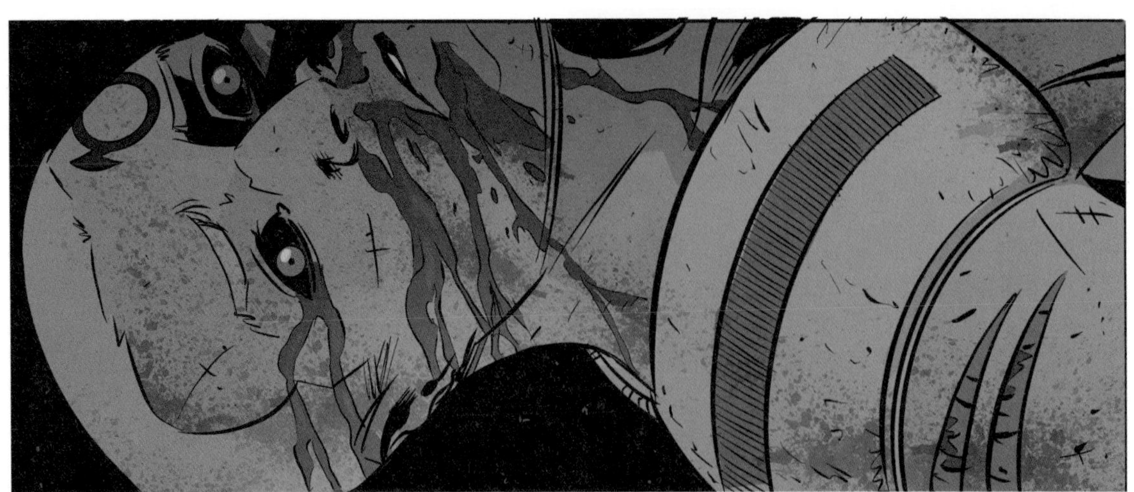

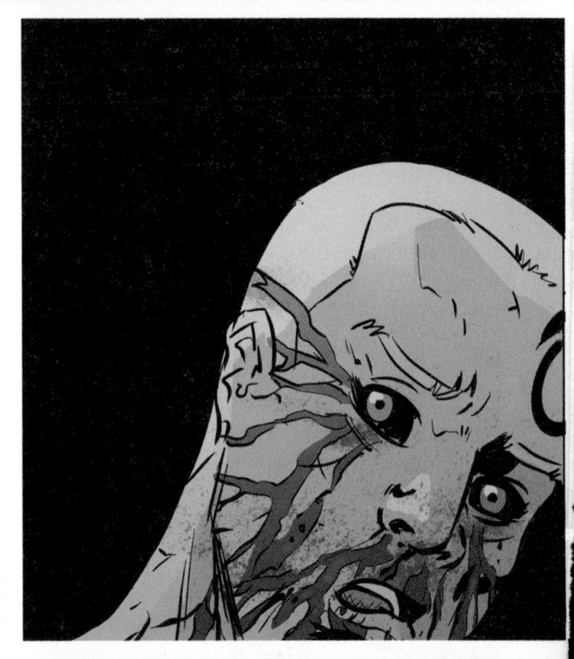

DEL?

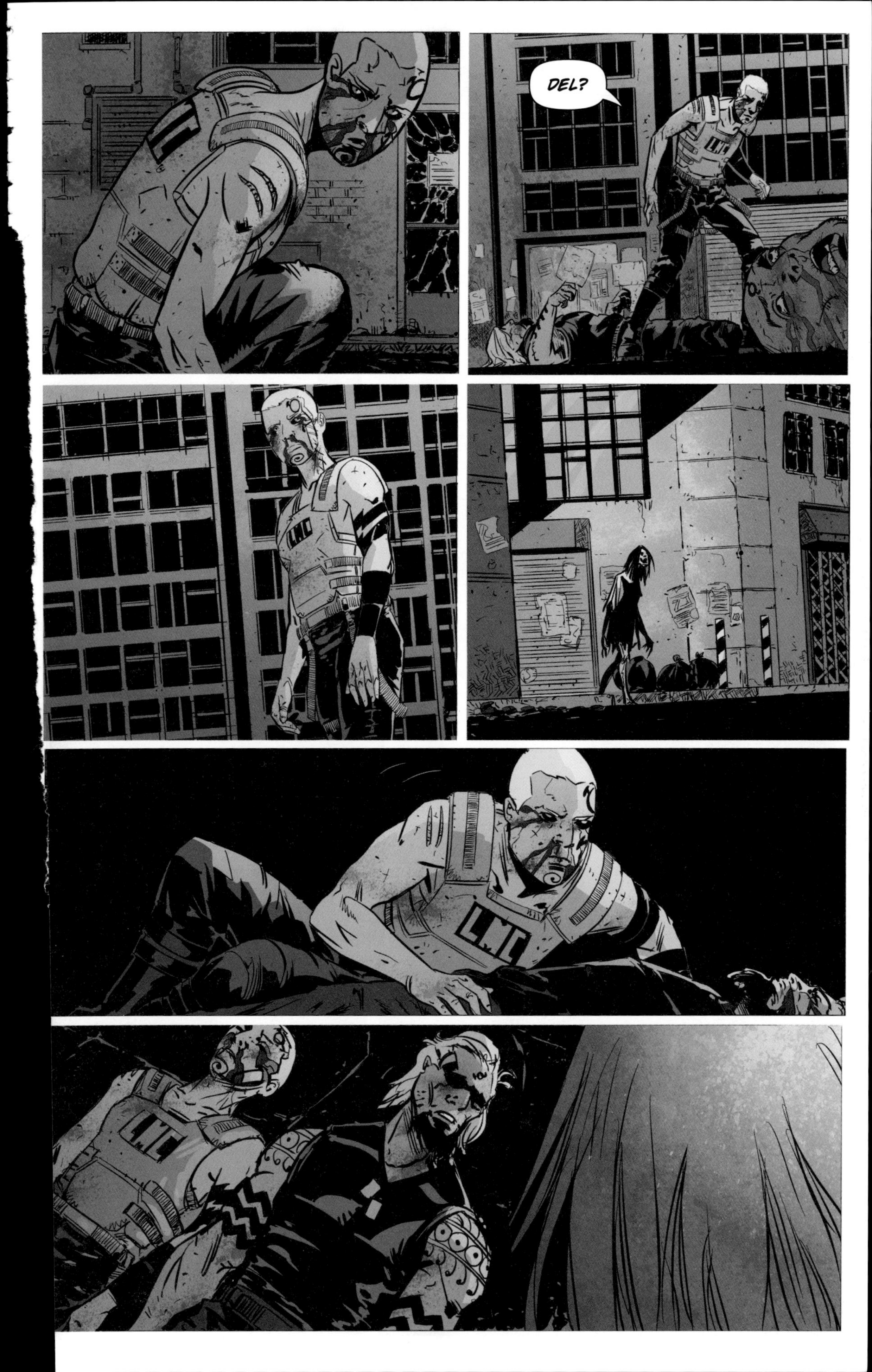
DEL?

SOMEONE ONCE ASKED ME IF I HAD FAITH,
IF I BELIEVED IN A HIGHER POWER.

I SAID I DID NOT.

BUT I WAS WRONG.

I DID BELIEVE, IN ONE THING.

I DID HAVE FAITH, IN ONE PERSON.

AND SHE WAS COMING FOR ME.

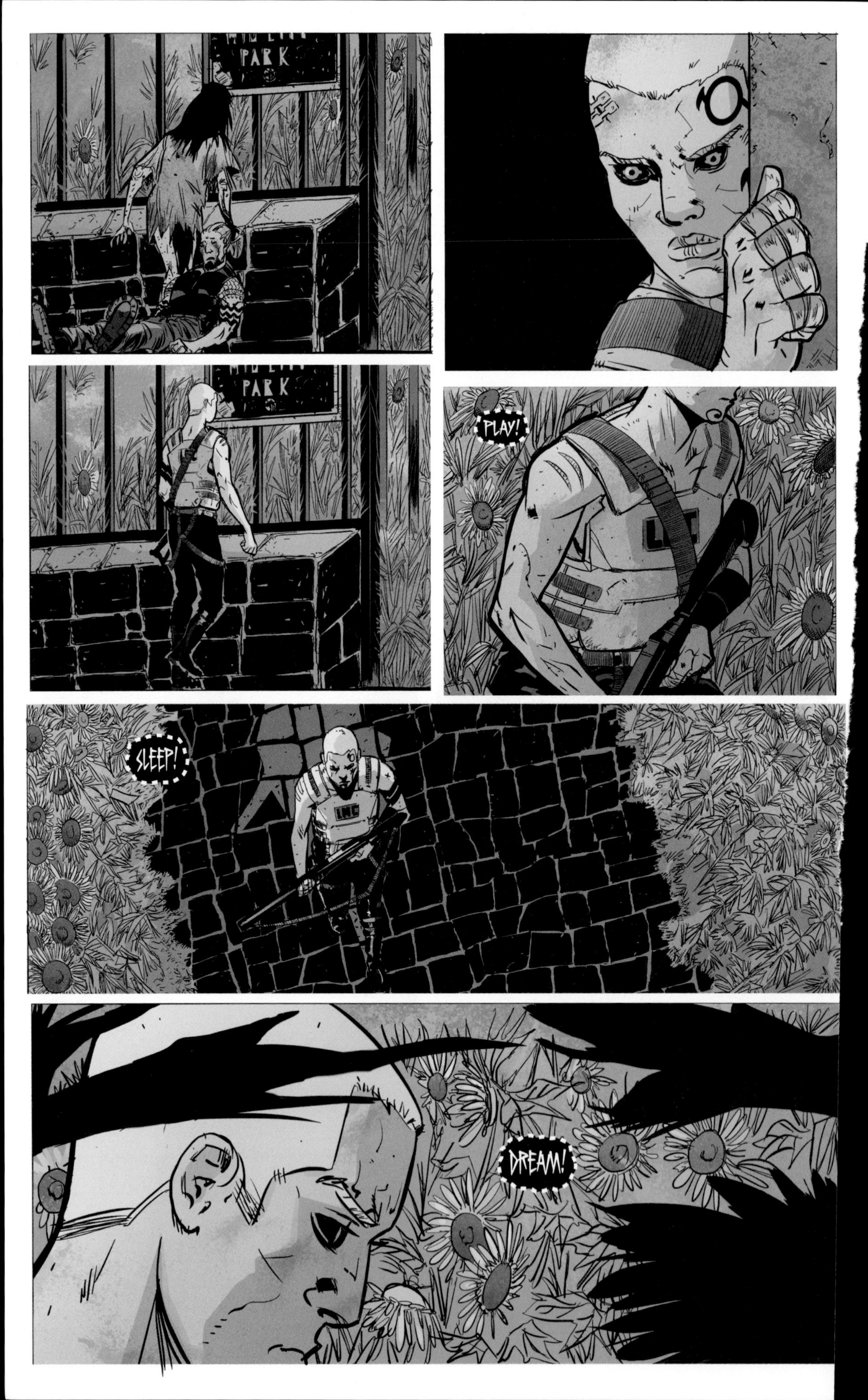
PARK
PARK
PLAY!
SLEEP!
DREAM!

PLAY!

SLEEP!

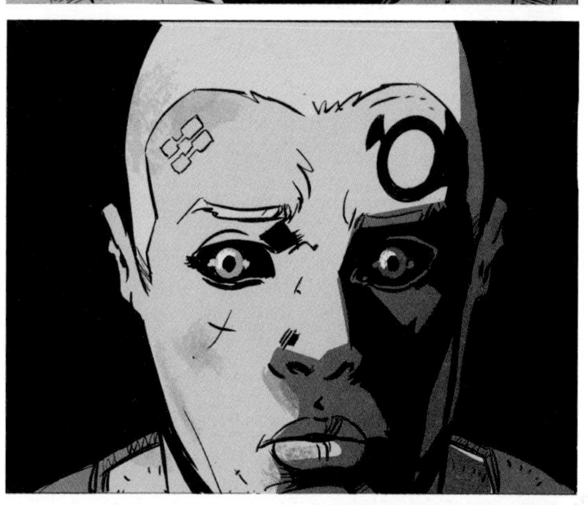

DREAM!

PLAY!

THUNDER

SLEEP!

DREAM!

THE *MILK*, THE *SACRED MILK*-

THE JUICE.
FUCK!
PLAY?

NO!

YOU UNDERSTAND WHAT THIS IS?!

THE GIRL!

OR I INCINERATE THIS WHOLE FUCKING BLOCK!

THE GIRL!

DEL?!

FALE GOT ME HOME LIKE SHE PROMISED.

BUT MY MIND HAD BEEN LEFT BEHIND, SOMEWHERE BEYOND THE WALLS OF ZONE 1.

FOR WEEKS I DREAMED.
Sonic Youth

MY AUNT TOOK CARE OF ME...

..FED ME, BATHED ME.

AND FALE WAS THERE, ALSO.
FALE, UNKNOWABLE, A KILLER OF MEN.

SHE CONSIDERED HER JOB INCOMPLETE.

SHE WATCHED OVER ME.
AND WAITED.

NOW...
NOW IS THE TIME. IT'S BEEN HOURS... DAYS.
SO TIRED.
I WILL NOT DIE HERE!

THIS WILL NOT KILL ME.
BETTER?
I WILL NOT DIE HERE!

ALMIGHTY
DEVELOPMENT

ALMIGHTY
DEVELOPMENT

DELETED SCENES

ALMIGHTY FIRST PASS

EARLY TAKE ON THE OPENING WITH A COMPLETELY DIFFERENT VERSION OF FALE

A L M I G H T Y

by Ken Nolan

FADE IN:

EXT. DESERTED CITY STREET - DAY

A broken child's doll lies face-down in the middle of cracked pavement.

PULLING BACK - the doll is surrounded by garbage, old car hulks, detritus from a formerly inhabited world.

BACK FURTHER - revealing a scarred, empty cityscape, windowless skyscrapers reaching skyward. Kudzu and weeds threaten to take back the city, vines everywhere.

An intersection where traffic used to flourish; dormant traffic lights like sullen, gargoyle-watchful eyes.

Finally, there is a sound in the empty city.

The distant whine of a precision engine. Grows in strength and volume. Closing in fast as --

-- A MASSIVE MOTORCYCLE TIRE runs over the doll.

The engine HOWLS as the machine blurs past, rider nimbly dodging car hulks and an old city bus.

The doll tumbles to the gutter, near an old KFC bucket.

THE DOLL -- one eye missing, one open, stares into doll-eternity. The mouth is a smudged hole, filled with dirt.

A mechanical voice inside, long dormant, plaintive:

DOLL
Mama... Mammma...

We CLOSE IN the eye becoming everything.

The sky is reflected in the green doll's eye.

Titles fall from the reflected sky:

ALMIGHTY

...And then blow away into the warren of downtown city streets, lifeless, forgotten.

The doll is left behind.

EXT. OFFICE BUILDING - DAY

A windowless, crumbling three-story office building stares back.

Before it is a half-destroyed, futuristic Abrams A-22 tank, hole blasted in its hull who knows how many years ago. Now the tank is graffiti-strewn, forgotten.

INT. OFFICE BUILDING - DAY

MOVING through the forgotten cubicles and abandoned work stations -- there are MEN, heavily tattooed, in various states of repose. Some asleep, others drug-dazed, eyes glassy, mouths half-open.

Two men watch a pirated feed of a baseball game, two unfamiliar teams playing in an enclosed stadium.

OUR VIEW moves down the hall, to a long, narrow corridor, ending at a room that reads: VAULT.

INT. OFFICE VAULT - DAY

Darkness...

...A few shafts of light, coming from a hole in the ceiling. And a sound, a young woman's voice, maybe 15, whispering in the dark:

YOUNG GIRL
I will not... I will not....

A squeak of something metal on metal.

YOUNG GIRL (CONT'D)
I will not.... I will --

The young girl's voice is ragged, weak.

YOUNG GIRL (CONT'D)
-- not die here...

ON THE YOUNG WOMAN'S EYES -- glimpsed in a sliver of pale sunlight coming through the ceiling. Green eyes. Desperate. Determined.

She whispers again --

YOUNG GIRL (CONT'D)
I will not die here.

The girl has been locked in a barred VAULT -- a place that once held security equipment, weapons, monitors. This place was an old FBI Office.

The vault is in neglect, its steel bars corroded, the main door leaning to one side off of a broken hinge. But it's still functional.

The girl has been locked inside, an old chain bike lock wrapped around the door to keep it secure.

IN THE DARKNESS -- the girl works with a half-broken screwdriver at a vault bar. She's been working on it for days, loosening the point where metal meets metal.

THE BAR -- moves back and forth, slightly. She's getting some purchase on the old, corroded joint.

She only uses one hand. The other is useless for now.

She gets enough leverage. Enough...

Crrrreeaaakkk. The bar foundation gives way with one final effort from the girl.

She YANKS at the bar with her good hand. Kicks at it. It starts to sway forward. Starts to give. Bending at the bottom. She grabs it and yanks it back and forth.

She's beyond hungry, exhausted, fingertips bloody from the work.

YOUNG GIRL
I will -- NOT --
(YANKS the wood)
DIE HERE.

The bar FALLS forward, clanking to the linoleum floor.

She's got about five and a half inches of space now.

Only now do we see that her left hand is heavily bandaged, blood seeping through.

She'll never fit through.

She tries. Her body wriggles through. So thin from days without food. But her head --

-- won't go. She pulls, twisting her skull.

Howls in pain. RIPS hair from her scalp, blood spurting. Her head POPS through the bars.

CONTINUED:

She's free from the vault.

INT. FBI BUILDING -- DAY

The girl opens the door to the vault room, just a crack. Her eye scans the hallway.

She opens the door another inch.

Ducks back when a rough-looking MOTORCYCLE GANG MEMBER walks past the door, heading toward --

-- the men's room.

She watches the man go inside.

Opens the door again. Sneaks out.

INT. FBI BUILDING - DAY

The girl has to crawl past GANG MEMBERS, one watching a portable TV with some kind of poorly-shot sitcom in it. The man snickers as he eats an from an old tuna fish container.

THE GIRL -- stays low, crawling at times, using the old office partitions as cover.

She makes it to --

-- THE STAIRWELL.

Opens the door, slips through the crack.

EXT. FBI BUILDING - DAY

The girl stumbles from the crumbling building's fire escape stairwell and out into --

-- SUNLIGHT.

The white hot blast of day nearly knocks her down.

The girl's name is DEL.

She might be 14 at most. Skinny, jeans ragged, shirt frayed on her scarecrow body. Her eyes are intelligent, quick, taking in her predicament in moments.

VOLUME TWO

IN THE

THIRD WORLD AMERICA SAGA

REMEMBER AMPHION

LAROCHE

ALMIGHTY LEADS TO THE FINAL SERIES IN THE THIRD WORLD AMERICA SAGA